P9-CPW-192

TRYOUT TROUBLE

Irene Punt

cover by
Ramón Pérez

interior images by
Jason Laudadio

Scholastic Canada Ltd.

Toronto New York London Auckland Sydney
Mexico City New Delhi Hong Kong Buenos Aires

Scholastic Canada Ltd.
604 King Street West, Toronto, Ontario M5V 1E1, Canada

Scholastic Inc.
557 Broadway, New York, NY 10012, USA

Scholastic Australia Pty Limited
PO Box 579, Gosford, NSW 2250, Australia

Scholastic New Zealand Limited
Private Bag 94407, Botany, Manukau 2163, New Zealand

Scholastic Children's Books
Euston House, 24 Eversholt Street, London NW1 1DB, UK

www.scholastic.ca

Library and Archives Canada Cataloguing in Publication
Punt, Irene, 1955-, author
Tryout trouble / Irene Punt ; cover illustration by Ramón
Pérez ; interior illustrations by Jason Laudadio.
ISBN 978-1-4431-3345-6 (pbk.)
I. Laudadio, Jason, 1970- , illustrator II. Title.
PS8581.U56T79 2014   jC813'.54   C2014-901825-8

Text copyright © 2014 by Irene Punt.
Illustrations copyright © 2014 by Scholastic Canada Ltd.

All rights reserved.
No part of this publication may be reproduced or stored in a retrieval system, or
transmitted in any form or by any means, electronic, mechanical, recording, or other-
wise, without written permission of the publisher, Scholastic Canada Ltd., 604 King
Street West, Toronto, Ontario M5V 1E1, Canada. In the case of photocopying or other
reprographic copying, a licence must be obtained from Access Copyright (Canadian
Copyright Licensing Agency), 1 Yonge Street, Suite 800, Toronto, Ontario M5E 1E5
(1-800-893-5777).

6 5 4 3 2 1   Printed in Canada 121   14 15 16 17 18

Contents

*To Dad and Lucy for our many
hours of storytelling*

Jitters

"It's going to be a happy hockey day!" announced Tom as he finished his lunch. Tom loved his team, the Glenlake Hawks. He loved playing centre with Mark on right wing, Stuart on defence and Jordan in goal. They were his best friends and they played best . . . together! School and a week of September tryouts were about to start, which made Tom feel anxious and excited at the same time. There was only one thing to do.

Tom grabbed his road hockey stick,

gloves and helmet. He headed toward Stuart's house, stickhandling a ball along the sidewalk. *TAP, TAP, TAP* . . .

TAP, TAP, TAP. He turned left. He turned right. He skilfully dodged a light pole. He tried to remember all the things Coach Howie had taught him. Head up. Deke,

without losing the ball. Focus. Be positive. Know the rules. Wear a jock!

When Tom looked ahead, he saw his buddies huddled around the net, waiting for him. "Woo hoo!" they yelled.

Mark was wearing polka-dot board shorts and neon sunglasses.

Stuart was wearing torn elbow pads.

Jordan was wearing his scary goalie face. "Grrmph!" he growled.

Tom ran with the ball, then took a quick shot at the net. The ball hit the crossbar and rebounded to Stuart. Stuart passed to Mark. Mark to Tom. Tom flicked the ball with a wrist shot and it bounced over Jordan's goalie blocker.

"Goal!" shouted Tom.

"Grrr," Jordan growled in frustration. He scooped the ball out of the net and slapped one to Mark.

Mark controlled the ball and chipped it to Tom. "That was my *gockey* shot. It's like golf + hockey = gockey. Get it?"

Everyone cracked up. Mark was the funniest kid they knew.

Stuart tripped over a pebble as he snuck up behind Tom. He stole the ball, took a slapshot, stumbled and scored! Stuart was the clumsiest kid they knew.

Jordan looked very worried. "Tryouts start this week and my nerves are fr-fr-fried." He slumped over his goalie stick. "I hate tryouts."

"Me, too," said Mark. "We have to compete against each other to get placed on a team. I say tryouts are *cry-outs*. I've seen the big guys bawl their eyes out."

Stuart covered his ears. "*Shhh!* Stop talking about tryouts! It gives me a rash."

"But. But. What if we don't make the same team?" Jordan frowned.

Tom had never thought of *that*. He and his best friends had been together for two seasons, on the same hockey team and in the same classroom at school. They were a team! They carpooled together. They practised together. They played shinny together. They worked *together*. They were HAWKS! And Coach Howie was *their* coach.

Tom shook his head. Listening to all this tryout nonsense was making a puck-sized lump in his stomach. "C'mon. We'll be together. It's a no-brainer. After all, we are in the same evaluation group!" He held out a gloved fist. Mark, Stuart and Jordan banged their fists on top.

Together they cheered, "HAWKS!"

Now everything was better.

Tom lunged for the ball with his stick. "Let's go!" he shouted. "Keep your head up!"

Mr. Watson's Garage

The road hockey game went on and on and on.

Tom scored six times.

Stuart scored three times for a hat trick.

Mark scored twice.

Jordan lifted his goalie mask and moaned, "Eleven goals! What's with me?" He kicked off his runners and pulled off his orange socks. "Maybe it's these new socks! I remember the last time I wore new socks. It was when we were playing against the Northland Bulldogs at a tournament. That number 66 scored on me! We lost. And I blew my shutout record!" Jordan made his ugliest goalie face yet.

"Oh, yeah," agreed Mark. "Old, stinky socks are much better."

Tom remembered that game, too. Number 66 was his friend Harty from Champs Hockey Camp a year ago. He had taught Harty his wicked slapshot, and Harty used it to score the winning goal. It was a *great* hockey moment.

"How about a time out?" hollered Mr. Watson, waving them over to his garage. "I've got slush drinks here!"

The boys put down their road hockey sticks and raced toward Mr. Watson. Mr. Watson lived next door to Stuart. He loved helping the boys with the outdoor rink during the winter. Today his garage was filled with big boxes. An old slush machine was sitting on top of the workbench, next to packing supplies. He poured them each a special strawberry slush.

"Thanks," said Tom, placing the cold cup on his hot cheek. "Having your own slush machine is the coolest."

"No, the coolest thing in the world was when Mr. Watson drove us to the Saddledome to see a Calgary Flames game last season!" said Jordan.

"Oh, yeah!" said Tom, remembering sitting in front row seats.

"Well . . . one day, you guys are going to make the NHL!" Mr. Watson chuckled and winked.

"NHL! NHL! NHL!" chanted the boys as they leapt in the air.

"I will be watching you play when I'm living in sunny Florida," said Mr. Watson. "On my big screen TV."

"What?" gasped Tom. "Are you *moving*?"

Mr. Watson nodded, yes. "'Fraid so. Mrs. Watson is tired of frostbite and wearing long underwear."

Weird, thought Tom, because he loved Calgary and couldn't wait for winter, with temperatures so cold that water froze into ice — and ice turned into outdoor hockey rinks. Tom gulped. He liked Mr. Watson. He had let them use water from his house to flood the outdoor rink across the street at Crescent Park. What would they do now?

As if Mr. Watson had read Tom's mind, he said, "Don't worry about the outdoor rink. I'm leaving behind all my hoses and snow shovels for you boys . . . to keep the rink in tip-top condition!" Then he pointed to the walls, plastered with hockey posters. Some of the posters were autographed by famous players. Others were advertisements for

Don Cherry's hockey videos. "I'd love to give you guys all these posters I collected while working at the television station . . ."

"Yes!" gasped the four boys, thrusting their arms into the air and dancing.

"But . . ." continued Mr. Watson, ma[...] the *time out* signal. "I can't."

The boys froze. "Huh?"

"Sorry, boys. We glued the posters to the wall with super-duper extra strength rubber cement. Unfortunately, they must stay in the garage. If I try to remove them, they'll be ripped to shreds."

"Oh, rats," sighed Tom, feeling super-duper extra bummed out. He took a closer look at the posters. "There's the Stanley Cup in Calgary!"

"This poster has all the Olympic goalies," said Jordan in awe. "And their helmets."

"Wayne Gretzky and Sidney Crosby are on the ceiling!" said Stuart, looking up.

Mr. Watson sighed as he cranked up the slush machine and crushed more ice cubes. *GRRR!* It rocked. *GRRR!*

"The people who bought this house *scored*

11

big time!" Mark told his friends. "I'd sleep in this garage and never shut my eyes."

"No kidding," sighed Tom, checking out the funny Don Cherry posters. He loved watching Don Cherry's hockey highlights and bloopers. Mr. Watson must have collected a gazillion of them.

Mr. Watson took a deep breath. "I am going to miss you guys and the Flames." Suddenly his face lit up. "Hey . . . the new family moves here in a few days. The boy is a real hockey nut. Maybe you'll become friends!"

"No way," whispered Mark. "That kid got all the good posters." He pointed to the slush machine. "I bet he gets that, too. I don't like him already."

As Mr. Watson waved goodbye, he said, "Go Hawks, go! Get yourselves up to speed! And don't forget about school!"

First Day

It was the first day of school, the biggest event of the year!

The schoolyard at Chinook Park School was buzzing with 518 kids looking tanned and shampooed. Tom ran straight to meet Mark, Stuart and Jordan at the monkey bars. It felt good to know where to go and what to do.

Stuart was wearing new runners. They were black, shiny and pinching his heels.

Mark's hair was gelled and spiked. "Do you like my *scare-do*?" he asked with a laugh.

Tom laughed, too. "Boo!" he said, playing along.

Jordan turned around to show off his backpack. A hawk was printed on the front. Its wings stretched upward and its talons were open, ready for pickup.

"Cool," said Tom. "I think the hawk is grabbing *us* and . . ." Before he finished the sentence, his eyes spied a familiar head of hair in the crowd. It was red and wavy. It was . . . Harty, his friend from Champs Hockey Camp!

"Over here!" Tom yelped, jumping up and waving to him.

"Who's that?" Stuart, Mark and Jordan chimed. They looked confused.

Tom was too busy flapping his arms to answer. His heart was racing, just like on game day.

The two boys rushed toward each other,

greeting with a high-five and a low-five. Harty crossed his arms into a big X. "Give me a high-ten!"

Tom crossed his arms into a big X and did a happy high-ten. "What are *you* doing here?" he asked in amazement.

"We moved to this neighbourhood," answered Harty with a big grin.

"You got a new house?"

"Yup! And . . . a new dad, new dog, new sisters, new grandpa, new cousins, new school . . . and a NEW HOCKEY TEAM to try out for." He looked a little sweaty as he rhymed off his list.

"Wow," said Tom. "I got new school supplies."

"Me, too," laughed Harty.

Suddenly, like a red goal light lighting up, Tom's brain sparked. "Did you guys buy Mr. Watson's house?"

"Yup! The moving truck is there right now."

"Holy moly!" Tom exclaimed. "That makes you Stuart's next door neighbour!" Tom turned to tell his friends . . . when the nine o'clock bell rang. Dr. Dean, the principal, opened the doors to the school.

"Welcome back, children!" she announced from her megaphone, but no one took any notice.

Then, just like last year and the year before, the megaphone sounded off like a screeching cat, *"Kzzkzzkzz!"* It lasted for thirteen seconds, forcing everyone to plug their ears and grimace.

Dr. Dean cleared her throat and came in loud and clear. "Thank you. Now, our teachers have their classroom lists. Please stand beside your grade number and listen for your name." She put on her sunglasses

and pointed to the giant signs on the walls.

As the mob ran to hear names, Tom held back. "C'mon!" he motioned to Harty. "Follow me."

"I hope we are in the same class," Harty said, wiping sweat off his forehead.

"Me, too."

Every teacher held a classroom list.

Tom waited and watched and listened for names. He held his crossed fingers in the air as Miss Lucy read her list. Lots of names went right over Tom's head, except, "Mark Boswell . . . Jordan Deerfoot . . . Tom Hiller . . ."

That's me! Go Hawks, go! Tom kept listening and hoping.

"Harty McBey . . ."

Tom's face lit up. *Yeah! Harty's in.* He looked over.

Harty looked happy.

Then Miss Lucy said, "Follow me, class." She flashed a big, friendly smile.

All the students on Miss Lucy's list followed her into the school.

All of Tom's best friends walked toward room number seven . . . except Stuart. He was left standing with a sad face, in his pinching, shiny black runners.

Oh, no, thought Tom, looking behind. *Poor Stuart. He's not in Miss Lucy's class this year. And I can't FIX that!* Tom gave Stuart a thumbs-up as he called back to him, "See you at recess! Ball hockey!"

Stuart forced a smile.

Breaking the Ice

Room number seven was colourful and filled with interesting things. Goldfish, a math centre, flashlights, iPads. There were 24 desks, pushed into six groups of four. Tom, Mark, Jordan and Harty raced for the quad closest to the electric pencil sharpener. They set down their school supplies and waited.

"This is my friend Harty from Champs Hockey Camp," said Tom. "We met a year ago."

"You look familiar," Mark said.

"Yes! From Centennial Arena," said Harty. "One time . . ."

Miss Lucy made the *shhh!* sign and waited for silence.

"Welcome to your new classroom!" said Miss Lucy as she wrote her name on the whiteboard. She dotted the letter *i* with a happy face. "I'm your teacher, Miss Lucy. Together, we are going to have an awesome year! Let's start right now!" She discussed classroom expectations. She handed out more school supply lists. She reviewed the weekly schedule.

Tom looked at the clock. It was only 9:30.

Miss Lucy looked at the clock, too. "Everyone stand up and jog on the spot!" she said in a perky voice. Her arms swung back and forth.

Suddenly the room was alive with giggles and snorts. *Mrs. Wong never did this!* thought Tom, remembering his old teacher.

Miss Lucy signalled the students to sit.

"Now, let's break the ice!" directed Miss Lucy. "Strike up a fun conversation with your group!"

"Did I hear *ice*?" Mark snickered. "C'mon, let's talk hockey!"

"I hate hockey tryouts," said Jordan.

Hmm, thought Tom. *My turn*. He looked

at Harty, who was quietly twitching in his seat. "Guess what? Harty's the fastest skater on ice." Tom did a thumbs-up.

Harty's face turned tomato red. "Ahh . . . mostly because I wear stakes, er . . . I mean . . . skates."

"Wait a minute. You *do* look familiar. What team are you on?" asked Mark.

"I used to be a dog," answered Harty.

"Huh?" Mark wrinkled his nose.

"Northland Bulldogs."

Jordan made his ugly goalie face. "Do you know that number 66?"

"Well, yeah," said Harty. "I wa—"

Tom quickly cut him off. "What team now?"

"I am turning into a bird," said Harty. "I am trying out with your Glenlake Hawks."

"Awesome!" Tom slapped a high-five with Harty.

"Tom and I played on the same line at

hockey camp," said Harty. "Tom centre, me right wing."

"Wait. Tom and I are on the same line. I am right wing. You can't take *my* position." Mark wagged his finger.

Harty made an embarrassed face.

"Man, oh man. This is why I hate tryouts," said Jordan.

"There are fifteen skaters on a team," Tom reminded everyone. He really liked Harty and wanted his friends to like him, too. What would it take to impress his friends? Suddenly he had a very good idea. "Harty moved into Mr. Watson's house!" he said.

"You got all those good goalie posters," moped Jordan.

"What about the awesome slush machine in the garage?" asked Mark. "We love slushy drinks!"

"My mom said that Mr. Watson didn't leave that slush machine for us," said Harty. "I think it might be . . ."

Miss Lucy clapped her hands loudly. "Okay, class! Time for more business." She explained the bathroom board. "Don't ask, just write your name on the BB and *GO!*"

"Wow!" said Mark. "Too bad Stuart's not here. He spends a lot of time in the bathroom."

Tom, Mark and Jordan looked at each other, all thinking the same thing. *Stuart, we miss you!*

Finally the recess bell rang and the boys ran out to find Stuart. He was already playing ball hockey with Mario.

"We are in Mr. Sandhu's class," said Stuart.

"Lucky you. My brother had Mr. Sandhu. He is awesome!" said Mark, doing a spin. "You get to blow up volcanoes in Science!"

"Whoa!" gasped Stuart and Mario, surprised.

Be careful! thought Tom. *When Stuart blows up stuff, he gets blown up, too!*

Tom picked up a stick and reached for the ball. Harty quickly stole it. He passed to

Mark. Mark ran with the ball, then tapped it back to Stuart. Harty stole the ball again. This time he flicked it right into the net.

"Woo hoo!" Harty shouted as the bell rang.

It's Just a Game

After school it was hockey tryouts and evaluations at Centennial Arena.

The cold lobby was buzzing with the second group of players and their parents.

"Yikes!" "What dressing room?" "Hurry!" "Where's Coach . . . ?" "My mouthguard!" "What time?" "Oh, no!" "I'm stoked!" "We're on!"

They were revved up and ready to be divided into teams. The big message board read:

NOVICE HAWKS
GROUP B ON NEXT
GOOD LUCK!

Mark rushed through the main arena door with a case of nervous giggles.

Stuart walked slowly, his body covered in blotches.

Harty arrived mumbling to himself.

Jordan dragged a huge goalie bag with his shaking hands. "I hate tryouts," he said to himself.

Tom took no notice of his friends. His stomach felt weird and his head was full of too many hockey tips. *Soft and fast hands. Cradle the puck. Head up. Shoot high. Shoot hard. Anticipate the play.* He trudged past the snack bar, under the bleachers, down the hall and into dressing room number three. Stuart limped alongside him.

"Blisters?" guessed Tom.

"Yeah, I shouldn't have worn new shoes," sighed Stuart, walking on tiptoes. "Now I have to put my skates on and I don't know how I am going to skate."

"Youch!" Tom could almost feel his pain.

— ● —

The dressing room was a madhouse as players layered their gear — a jock, shin pads, hockey socks, sock tape, padded pants, skates, shoulder pads, elbow pads, neck guard, practice jersey and a numbered pinny. Then every player snapped on a helmet, popped in a mouthguard, pulled down a face mask, put on gloves and grabbed his hockey stick.

Coach Howie walked through the door. "Hi, guys!" he said, quieting the room. He took off his Hawks cap.

Tom sat up and listened.

"Welcome back, Hawks! And a warm welcome to our new players. For those of you who don't know me, I am Coach Howie, one of the six coaches running the evaluations. Last year I coached Team Four."

"Yeah!" Everyone from last year's Team Four, including Tom and his friends, cheered.

Coach Howie held up his hand. "The next seven days are going to be crazy. We have over a hundred players to place on six Novice teams. We have three evaluation groups."

Fifteen skaters and two goalies will make a team, thought Tom, doing the math. *Thirty-four in each evaluation group.*

Coach Howie said, "Before you head out onto the ice, in front of the evaluators, I want you to THINK about one big question: WHY? Why do you play minor hockey?"

"NHL!" someone shouted out.

Coach Howie smiled, but didn't respond.

Tom thought about his answer. He loved the game of hockey. He loved playing with his friends. He loved being part of a team. "It's fun!" Tom exclaimed.

"Right on!" said Coach Howie. He taped a Hockey Canada poster to the wall. The caption read, *RELAX! IT'S JUST A GAME!*

"Now get out there, forget about the evaluators and just try your best!" said Coach Howie.

The door opened.

Mark turned to Stuart, Jordan and Tom. Each boy put out a gloved fist and banged one on top of another, ending with a loud yelp, "Hawks!"

Tom looked at Harty and said, "Let's work extra hard out there, like when we were at Champs Hockey Camp!"

"You're on!" said Harty.

"Here we go!" announced Tom, heading for the freshly flooded ice. A smile spread across his face.

First Evaluation

Tom took long, slow strides while bending and stretching to warm up. The coaches stood at centre ice. The evaluators sat in the stands, holding clipboards and pens. Their eyes followed the skaters as they began gliding around the rink. Tom broke into a swift pace.

A whistle blew. Tom listened.

"Skate forward. We're watching your crossovers," shouted a coach.

As Tom cruised by the scorekeeper's box, Harty passed him and took the corner with ease. *Hmm. Nice.* Seeing that, Tom concentrated. He pushed hard and sped up. He looked into his turn, led with his stick, kept his shoulders up. The toe of his blade hit the ice first as he stepped over and over and over — pushing with his edges. *SWOOSH. SWOOSH.* He took the corner beautifully. His crossovers were nearly perfect.

"Faster!" shouted a coach.

Tom looked ahead. He caught a glimpse of Mark. His left shoulder drooped and his skates were hitting the ice heel first.

OH, NO! thought Tom.

"Now skate backwards!" hollered a coach.

Determined, Tom pivoted and turned.

Stuart tripped over his feet and thumped bum-first into the boards. Twice.

OH, NO! thought Tom.

Jordan crouched between the pipes as a goalie coach took shots on net. Jordan swatted

the flying pucks with his big goalie stick.
"Grrmph!" he growled, making his scary goalie
face. Four pucks swirled around his feet.

OH, NO! thought Tom.

———•———

"Everyone against the boards," ordered
Coach Howie. "Quick stops and starts
across the ice! Four times!"

"Faster!"

"Now back to the boards!"

The coaches skated past the skaters, taking note of who was tired and winded.

Tom felt great, but some skaters were red-faced, slouched and gasping for air. He checked out his friends. They all looked good following *this* drill. Summer road hockey had paid off for them.

The evaluation moved on to stickhandling, passing and shooting. The last fifteen minutes were game time.

Little reminders kept popping into Tom's head. *Look where you're passing. Soft hands. Don't shoot at the goalie. Follow the shot for a rebound.*

Tom glanced up at the stands. The evaluators barely smiled as they took notes. Tom decided to stop worrying about them and keep trying his best. It was just too hard to worry and work at the same time.

On Tom's last shift he won the killer faceoff. He blazed down the ice, steering the puck toward the net. He passed to Mark — Mark to Harty — Harty to Tom. He caught the puck, swooped in front of the net and scored! *YES!* Tom felt pumped.

At the end of the hour, the buzzer sounded and everyone cleared the ice for the next group of skaters — Group A.

—— • ——

Back in the dressing room, Mark was squirting his water bottle over his head.

"That evaluation was a doozy! I don't feel like a Hawk any more. I feel like a dead duck!" He laughed at his own joke.

Stuart was close to tears. "My feet. My

39

feet. Ooh-aah." He unlaced his skates and carefully pulled them off.

Jordan looked happy. "I was good . . . 'cause I wore my oldest and stinkiest socks."

I feel pretty good, too, thought Tom. *I kept my head up. I focused. I showed them my wicked slapshot.* He smiled.

"Hey, guys!" Mark called out. "Who knows this one?" He held up his pointer finger and the song broke loose.

> *One, two, three, four,*
> *C'mon Hawks, shoot and score!*
> *Five, six, seven, eight,*
> *We are Hawks, we are great!*
> *One, two, three, four,*
> *C'mon Hawks, score some more!*
> *Five, six, seven, eight,*
> *Win those games, we can't wait!*

"Go Hawks, go!" howled Mark, flapping his arms and wiggling his bottom.

Harty sat off to the side, not knowing the

40

cheer and looking awkward. He tore the sock tape off his socks and layered it onto the giant tape-ball he kept in his hockey bag. He seemed sad.

Tom looked at Harty.

"Whoa!" Tom interrupted everyone. "Check out Harty's monster tape-ball! I bet it weighs a hundred kilos!" He picked it up with a fake struggle. "Umph!"

"Let me try!" "Let me see!" "I'm next!" said the group.

"I've got two seasons . . . or . . . over fifty games of sock tape in this ball," Harty said, proudly. "From when I played for the . . ." He stopped before saying, *Northland Bulldogs*. He looked around. Everyone was a happy Glenlake Hawk. He wanted to be one, too.

Band-Aid Buddies

Coach Howie entered the dressing room carrying a case of sports drinks. "Here, guys. Free samples of Grape Guzzle! I got them from work." Coach Howie was always bringing in samples from the Smokin' Cola Company. Mark piped up, reciting the TV commercial: "Great Grape Guzzle! is so DELICIOUS, it's RIDICULOUS!" *BURP!*

Everyone laughed. Mark took a bow.

"Enough, Mark," said Coach Howie. He looked tired. "Here's what's next. Go home and sleep. You will receive an e-mail tomorrow telling you what time your next evaluation is. Don't be alarmed if you are asked to join Group A or C. Don't think of it as being moved up or down. Just think of it as being moved *around*. The coaches and evaluators are trying their best to place you on a team where you will play the most hockey . . . and have the most fun! See you in two days."

One by one, players exited the dressing room looking pooped. Jordan and Mark gave a salute as they left to catch their rides.

Stuart sat on the bench, nearly a zombie. "First day of school: not so good. First day of tryouts: not so good. First day wearing new shoes: BAD IDEA!"

As Tom struggled to unknot his skate laces, he told Stuart what his grandma always said: "Things will get better. And tomorrow will be a better day."

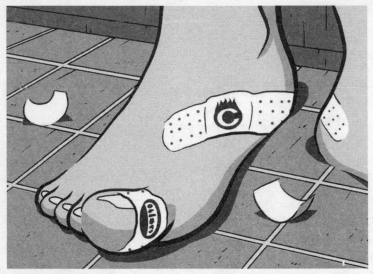

"Yeah, right." Stuart huffed and rolled his eyes. "Easy for you to say."

"Wait a minute!" Harty reached into his hockey bag. "Here. Want these?" He held out a box of Band-Aids. They had NHL team logos printed on them.

Stuart's eyes widened. "Wowzers! I love these!" He peeled them open and stuck the Calgary Flames on his biggest blister. The Edmonton Oilers went around his big toe.

The Toronto Maple Leafs covered his left heel.

"They work best when you double them up," instructed Harty.

"You get blisters, too?" Stuart asked.

"Yup. Big, juicy ones that pop water and then look like strawberries." Harty frowned.

"Whoa!" said Stuart. "We could be blister buddies."

"Oh, yeah!" laughed Harty, his face lighting up. He removed his socks and showed Stuart a scar shaped like a mouthguard.

Stuart clapped. "That's a keeper."

"I'm going to *love* being your neighbour!" said Harty. "We can walk to school together."

"Yes!" said Stuart, jumping up. He bumped his head. "Ouch! At least I have Band-Aids so I can walk again."

Tom watched Stuart and Harty, happily

Band-Aiding. *Hmm. I'm usually the one making Stuart feel better.*

Harty and Stuart did a high-five and a low-five. Then Harty made an X with his arms. "C'mon Stu! Give me a high-ten!" he said.

Tom's heart sank. He had never been jealous of scrapes, scabs, blisters, bumps, bruises and Band-Aids before. But he was today.

Two Day

Tom walked slowly to school. Every muscle in his body ached. He scrunched his shoulders. His backpack felt like he was piggybacking a hippopotamus.

He saw Harty, hanging out with Jordan, by the swings. They were practising their scary faces.

Jordan did his usual scary goalie face. "Grrmph!"

"You look amazing!" complimented Harty. "Now try this one." He wrinkled his forehead, gnashed his teeth and snarled like a raging pit bull, "Garrrrgh!"

"Good one!" said Jordan. He concentrated. He copied Harty's ugly face and did a much bigger growl. "GarrAWWW!"

Harty shook his whole body and chattered his teeth. "See how scared I am? Your look is NHL material!"

Tom couldn't help frowning. He had never been jealous of Jordan's ugly face before, but he was now.

"Jordan, I have an idea!" said Harty. "You would look fearless if you drew fangs on your goalie helmet." He reached into his backpack and pulled out his new felt markers. "I can help you. And if you come over to my garage we can check out the NHL posters for ideas."

Jordan's face went from ugly to super happy. "Yes! Yes! Yes!" He jumped from one foot to the other, his arms flailing in the air. "You are the best! I think my hockey tryout jitters are gone!"

Tom stood by watching. He felt invisible to Jordan and Harty. *Hmm*, Tom thought. *I'm usually the one teaching stuff to Jordan.* Harty was starting to bug him — big time.

————●————

The bell rang and the playground emptied as students streamed into the school.

Miss Lucy swung door number seven open.

"Good morning, class! Welcome to day number two!" Her hair was in two pigtails, and she was wearing two name tags, two watches and two  pairs of glasses. "Find your seats."

The desks were pushed into twos. Mark and Harty were a pair. Jordan and Raj were, too. Tom found his desk. He was Kylie's partner. She was wearing pink butterflies in her hair.

"Today we are learning about words that are spelled the same but have two completely different meanings," said Miss Lucy. "They are called *homographs*."

"Like the word . . . *rose*?" Kylie asked eagerly. "I *rose* from my soft purple chair. And a yellow *rose* is a beautiful flower."

"Yes! Exactly! See how many you can

think of with your partner," said Miss Lucy. "I have a surprise for the winners!"

Immediately, Kylie began to make a list. She was like a homograph machine, spitting out *fly, rock, pop, duck, boot, bat, tip, bank, ball, sock.* She looked at Tom. "C'mon, think! Two brains are better than one!"

"Stick," offered Tom.

"Is hockey the *only* thing you think about?" asked Kylie. "Hockey, hockey, hockey."

"Pretty much," said Tom. He looked over at Mark and Harty. They were having two hundred times more fun with homographs.

"*Toot*," joked Mark. "*Toot* sounds like a two word! The train *toots*. And I *toot* after eating chili!"

Mark and Harty cracked up.

"*Sport!*" howled Mark, with tears running down his cheeks. "You are a good *sport*. And we play a *sport* — HOCKEY!"

Hmm, thought Tom. *I am usually the one joking around with Mark and helping his punchlines.* But today, Tom felt like the *boring guy*.

"Mark, do you want to watch some Don Cherry videos at my house?" said Harty. "The bloopers are the funniest hockey moves in history."

Tom's heart sank to his runners. *I wanted my friends to like Harty . . . but not more than they like me!*

"Hey, Tom. We need more words," said Kylie, snapping her fingers.

"Puff!" said Tom. He thought, *I am watching Mark puff up. And in a puff, my Hawks are off — without me.*

"Puff is a nice word," agreed Kylie, and she added it to the list.

Tom sniffed back a secret tear.

As Kylie worked on their list, Tom wrote

his name on the BB and left the class. Maybe he would see Stuart in the bathroom. He'd have a tissue.

A New Cookie

Tom trudged home, alone and grumpy. He headed directly for his backyard.

A practice stick and pucks were scattered on the walk. Giant truck tires leaned against the brick wall. Tom grabbed his stick and took a few shots at the tire targets. *Bang! Bang! Bang!* Right into the centre of the tires.

Rap! Rap! Rap! Dad knocked on the kitchen window. "Hey, Tom!"

"Hi, Dad!" yelled Tom. "Did you get an e-mail with my evaluation time?"

"No, not yet." shouted his dad.

"No?" Tom headed for the kitchen. Dad was shuffling cookies from the oven to a cooling rack.

"Hey," said Dad, looking up. "What's up? What did you learn at school today?"

"Number two," answered Tom.

"Number two?" Dad had a crooked smile on his face.

"Yeah. We did number two." Tom rolled his eyes and grinned. "That's when Kylie and I won the word contest prize. We get to feed the goldfish twice this week."

"Awesome!" said Dad with a high-five.

Yeah, thought Tom. *It feels good to win. Kylie was a pretty good partner after all. She really challenged me.* He grabbed a cookie. "Huh?" Tom looked carefully. It was brown with slimy green bits.

"I just invented the chocolate dill pickle

cookie," said Dad, proudly. "C'mon, try it . . . a new mix. You love chocolate and dill pickles. Why not together?"

"Okay." Tom liked the way his dad did crazy things. He closed his eyes and bit into the gooey, warm cookie. It felt weird in his mouth and tasted a little odd. He tried another bite. "You know . . . the more I eat, the better it gets." Tom smiled and reached for another cookie. "Mmm. These could become my new favourite cookies! Maybe even the *world's best*!"

"*Shhh!* Don't tell your mom that! She'll be hurt and jealous."

"What? That's crazy," said Tom.

"Well, nobody likes to feel replaced. And Mom fancies herself the cookie boss here." Dad winked.

Tom thought back. He had felt replaced all day and it didn't feel so good. "Would Mom be mad if I liked *both* of your cookies? Like a tied game with no winner or loser?"

"I think that would be perfectly fine," said Dad. "After all, there is room for two good cookies in the world. And a little competition makes you try harder."

Tom downed a glass of milk. *RRRING!* He jumped to answer the phone. It was Jordan looking for a ride to the next Group B evaluation at four o'clock the following day. "I hate tryouts," he reminded Tom.

RRRING! Mark was in Group B.

RRRING! Stuart was in Group C at six o'clock!

"Oh, no," Tom told Dad. "This is not good. What if we are not on the same team this season?"

"Well, it could happen," said Dad. "There are lots of players moving up a division. The coaches and evaluators have a big job placing players. Most of them have the exact same skills."

Tom held the phone in his hand, waiting for more calls.

Ding! Ding! The computer chimed with a new e-mail from Glenlake Hockey. Tom opened the e-mail and read:

You are now in the Novice Group A evaluation. Centennial Arena tomorrow at 5 o'clock.

Tom panicked. "I'm in the A group! That's usually the Team One and Two group! I have always played on a Team Four!"

"You have worked hard," said Dad. "You are a good team player. You take the game seriously. You play with heart. So I think you are ready for the challenge."

Tom felt like he had swallowed a puck. This news felt good and scary at the same time. *Teams One and Two! Wowzers! But . . . but . . .* "What if I totally mess up?"

"Thomas Hiller! You give it your best shot. And remember . . . anyone can have a blooper!" said Dad.

RRRING! It was Harty. He was in Group A, too. And he was trying out for the same position as Tom, CENTRE.

Team Players

Centennial Arena. Four thirty. Novice tryouts.

Tom stood by the spectator glass watching Group B battle for the puck in a fast-moving game. Jordan was in goal. Mark was right wing. They were on opposing teams — red pinnies versus green pinnies.

Mark caught a pass from his green defenceman. He guided the puck along the boards then crossed the ice. He passed to his centre.

Jordan skated forward, shifting his stick

to a blocking position. He made his ugly goalie face with his eyes glued to the puck. "Grrmph!"

THWAP! Jordan stopped the first shot. Mark caught the rebound and circled back, gaining control. *THWAP!* Mark's shot was crisp. But Jordan stopped the puck again, this time with his glove. The puck slid to Jordan's red defenceman. He passed it to open ice.

Bad play on defence, thought Tom.

Mark raced for the puck, picked it up on the end of his stick and took a giant slapshot. *PING!* The puck soared over Jordan's shoulder . . . into the net!

"Yahoo!" Mark cheered, holding his stick above his head.

"Way to go, Mark!" shouted Tom.

"Way to go, Mark!" echoed Harty. "You are awesome! Hang in there, Jordan! You rock!"

Mark and Jordan looked over and smiled.
Oh, boy. Here we go again! thought Tom.
It had been another long day at school with

Harty stealing his friends. Harty burped the longest burp with Mark. Harty drew the scariest picture with Jordan. Harty got the blackest bruise with Stuart. And Harty won the Day Three three-letter-word competition with Kylie. Tom shook his head. *Will this guy ever stop?*

"Hey, Tom," Harty whispered. "Are you ready for Goop A? Er . . . I mean Group A?"

Tom ignored him. He watched more hockey.

Harty shrugged and frowned. "I really miss my old friends and Bulldogs. My life *was* easy peasy, and now everything is new." He took a deep breath. "Including Mark, Jordan and Stuart."

Tom was not ready to speak.

Harty pushed on. "Thanks for sharing all your friends with me. I was super freaked out about moving to Chinook Park. But you made it easy for me." Harty tapped his stick. "Mr. Watson was right."

After the longest silence ever, Tom raised an eyebrow and asked, "What did Mr. Watson say?"

"That you guys are the best. That you have more fun than a barrel of monkeys. That you look after each other," said Harty. "You are team players through and through."

Tom blushed. Mr. Watson's words had stung. *Being a team player is the most important thing. It means being unselfish, sharing, trying your best. Oh, boy.* Tom felt guilty. He had not been the best to Harty just now. *Why is sharing your best friends so difficult?*

Harty continued, "Mr. Watson also said

that I am to share all the old hockey stuff he left in the garage. He gave me a heads-up on what you guys would like: pads for Stuart, NHL stuff for Jordan, funny videos for Mark. Next time you get a drive over, you get the slush drink machine. Mr. Watson said that you would know exactly what to do with it."

"Whoa! Me? I get my own slush machine!" exclaimed Tom. "Mr. Watson is so cool, he's frozen!"

Tom looked at Harty, who had tried his best — all week, in every way. "I'm glad you moved to Chinook Park. You are like a new cookie. Different, but good."

"Huh?" Harty laughed.

Tom crossed his arms into an X and they clapped a high-ten.

Group A

Soon the arena was buzzing with more players. Tom didn't recognize anyone.

"I'm so nervous for the Group A evaluation. What about you?" whispered Harty.

"Me, too," said Tom, his stomach knotted. "It's scary."

"Do you think we could both be centres on the same team?" asked Harty.

Tom thought about it. There is only one centre per line. But every team has three lines. It *would* be nice to have Harty on his team. "Anything is possible," said Tom.

Suddenly he felt better thinking they'd be together.

"Hi, guys!" It was Coach Howie. He was holding a large case of Lucky Lemon Guzzle. "Here, take one of these drinks for after your evaluation. Now you'd better get going. Suit up for Group A!" Coach Howie looked proud as he patted them on their backs.

"What if we both make Team One?" asked Harty.

"Ahh!" gasped Tom, choking. He opened his drink and guzzled it back all at once.

Harty did the same thing. Then together they let out the biggest *BURRRP!*

———•———

At five o'clock the new evaluators studied Group A. They were on the lookout for forehand, backhand, tape-to-tape passes, position, puck control, speed, strength, endurance, attitude, effort and sportsmanship.

At 5:30 everyone stopped for a water break. Tom finished off his water bottle and got it refilled. So did Harty.

"Whoa! Holy smokes," Tom told Harty. "Group A is way faster than Group B. Everything is electric! The passes, skating, plays, coaches' calls . . ."

"I sure don't feel like the fastest skater any more!" admitted Harty. "But I am pushing myself hard."

"Me, too," said Tom. He took another gulp of water.

They headed to the bench, ready to play a fifteen-minute game. Purple pinnies against white pinnies. Tom and Harty wore purple ones.

On Tom's first shift, he missed the faceoff.

On the second shift, Tom won the faceoff. He slapped the puck back to the defenceman and charged for the blue line. *OH, NO! He shouldn't be there!* The puck was turned over to the white pinnies. Their left winger passed to his centre. The centre barrelled down the ice in a breakaway, took a shot, SCORED!

Back on the bench, the coach said, "Tom and Harty, next shift I'm going to put you guys together, as wingers. Tom left wing. Harty right wing."

"Okay," they said.

"Weird," whispered Tom.

On the third shift, Tom and Harty filed onto the ice. Tom grabbed the puck. He faked left and went right for a perfect deke. Tom looked to Harty for a pass. Harty's head was out of position. One shoulder was dropped. He was slightly bent over and his knees were knocking together. A white pinny was closing in on Tom. Tom passed to his defenceman. The puck came back to Tom.

Suddenly Tom realized what was wrong with Harty. He had to go pee! Tom skated back down the ice and . . . oh, no . . . it hit him. Tom had to go, too! Youch! He couldn't

balance and his knees started knocking together. His skating went from long, smooth strides to little baby steps with his heels. His crossovers were over.

Harty was now in worse shape. His face purpled, just like his pinny.

Together they got out of the play and off the ice.

———●———

Back in the dressing room, Tom sat on the bench like a deflated balloon. Noise and laughter circled around him.

"I guess we are the Purple Pee Guys," Harty whispered with a crooked smile.

Tom brightened. "A couple of big bloopers," he whispered back. "Drinking that Lucky Lemon Guzzle before our evaluation was *bad* luck!"

They both laughed.

"We will never forget today," they said together. "Jinx!"

Coach Alex entered the dressing room. "Hi, guys!" he said, quieting the room. "You have one more evaluation and then you are on your team! Check your e-mail! Now, go home and get rested up." He set down a case of Lucky Lemon Guzzle by the door. "Grab a refreshment on your way out! Courtesy of Coach Howie!"

When Tom reached the long hallway, he spied Stuart, dressed and ready for the Group C evaluation. His face was covered in blotches and he was wearing enormous shoulder pads.

"You look like serious defence!" complimented Tom.

"Thanks!" Stuart beamed. "And those NHL Band-Aids make my feet feel great. I'm ready! Bring it on!"

"Yeah! Good luck out there!" Tom and Harty told him. They swigged back their drinks.

"Thanks," said Stuart. He frowned. "Lucky you guys. You got a drink! It took me so long to get my gear and Band-Aids on, I missed out! It's not fair. Everyone in Group C guzzled a Guzzle, but me!"

"Whoops," said Harty. "You might be the lucky one. I have a feeling that you are going to ace this evaluation!"

Tom looked up into the stands where the evaluators were taking notes. *I wonder which team or teams we will all end up on.*

"Hey, Stu . . . just try your best!" Tom said.

Team Photos

Finally a week of tryouts was O-V-E-R!

Tom sat on a stool in his kitchen, with new school supplies, finishing homework. He was to write about his week as if he was a news reporter. He sharpened his hockey stick pencil and wrote the hockey highlights first.

Stuart Vickers looked like a hockey pro in Group C!
Mark Boswell and Jordan Deerfoot were solid players in Group B!
Harty McBey and Tom Hiller were bloopered out of Group A!
Coach Howie returns to coach!
There is a new cookie in town!

Mom placed a cold glass of milk and a plate of Raisin Bran cookies in front of Tom. "I am glad this week is over," she said. "Now we can get on with a fun season. I hate tryouts."

—— ● ——

Six o'clock. Centennial Arena was buzzing. All six Glenlake Novice teams were dressed in gear and ready for their team photos.

Coach Howie held a megaphone. "Congratulations, Hawks! A new season is about to begin!" Then, just like last year and the year before, the megaphone sounded off like a screeching cat, "*Kzzkzzkzz!*" Everyone plugged their ears and grimaced. Finally Coach Howie came in loud and clear. "Now . . . please stand with your coach and your team."

Tom stood with his teammates, huddled

around their coach, Coach Howie. Besides him, there was Harty, Mark, Jordan, Stuart and twelve more. *They* were officially Team Three. "Woo hoo!" they hooted.

Tom glanced at his four best friends.

Mark looked happy, as if he'd just told a zinger of a joke.

Stuart's blotches were gone.

Harty blabbed with everyone about everything. His words were fast. "New hawks new house new sisters new hockey new school new dog new skates . . ."

Jordan made his happy goalie face. "Tryouts were okay," he mumbled.

Tom felt proud wearing his new Glenlake Hawks jersey. *Tryout troubles are over,* he thought. *Today is a better day!*

The photographer motioned where to go.

As the five boys moved into their positions on the chairs, Coach Howie said, "Smile for the camera! Don't worry about your hair! We're not peacocks, we're HAWKS!"

Everyone laughed.

"Click!" The photographer snapped a photo. It was just about perfect. Except . . . Mark's jersey was inside out, Stuart sneezed, Jordan looked down, Harty's mouth was open and Tom's mind was wandering. He was having visions of winning Calgary Minor Hockey Week and even the City Championships . . . this year for sure! Suddenly he was blasted out of his daze when Coach Howie announced, "Okay, team, we've got twenty minutes of ice time! Let's get out there and scrimmage! Get those new jerseys stinky!"

"Let's go!" shouted the team.

Team Three scrambled through the gate onto the ice. The two goalies set up in net. The fifteen skaters took turns playing out. The puck zoomed end to end. Players passed, passed, passed to their teammates. *I love hockey! I love being a Hawk!* thought Tom, with a warm feeling inside.

Finally Tom, Harty, Stuart, Mark and Jordan ended up on the ice at the same time. They set up: Jordan in goal, Tom at centre, Harty and Mark wingers, Stuart on defence.

Tom won the tricky faceoff. He shot the puck back to Stuart. Stuart grabbed the puck and knocked it along the boards. Mark picked up the puck and passed it to Harty. Harty to Tom. Tom back to Harty. Harty blazed down the ice on a breakaway. He wound up and blasted a wicked slapshot . . . right into the net.

"Yippee!" yelled Tom, followed by, "Oh, no!"

Everyone ended up in a dog pile in the net.

They picked themselves up and gave a quick group hug. They pumped their arms and raised their sticks while skating back to the bench. When Tom looked through the spectator glass, he saw Harty's family. They were cheering like crazy. It was the cheer Mark sang in the dressing room.

One, two, three, four,
C'mon Hawks, shoot and score!
Five, six, seven, eight,
We are Hawks, we are great!
One, two, three, four,
C'mon Hawks, score some more!
Five, six, seven, eight,
Win those games, we can't wait!
GO HAWKS, GO!

Suddenly Tom knew exactly what to do with the slush machine from Mr. Watson . . . have a "Welcome to Chinook Park" party for Harty's family. He began to think. *Maybe in Harty's garage! With the NHL players all around. After all, the more hockey, the better!*

If you liked this book, look for these other books about Tom and his friends.

ISBN 987-0-439-94897-5

Tom isn't so sure he wants to go to hockey camp without his friends — even though he loves hockey more than anything. But the coach is great, the drills are fun and before long, he's made a new friend. When Harty has trouble with his shots, Tom offers some advice. Will it make a difference?

ISBN 987-0-545-99681-5

The Glenlake Hawks are having a great hockey season — on the ice and in the dressing room. Tom and his friends take some of their team spirit to the classroom and the schoolyard. But after a funny presentation in the class they are sent to the principal's office. Can the boys use hockey teamwork to save the day?

ISBN 987-0-545-99765-2

Tom really likes his babysitter, Jeff. So do his friends. Jeff plays road hockey with them after school, and now he's a referee at the local arena. But when he calls penalties against their team, the boys get mad and say things they regret. Can Tom and his friends patch up the mess and play by the rules?

ISBN 987-1-4431-0442-5

Tom loves playing hockey with his friends on the Glenlake Hawks. When he suggests using an outdoor rink for their annual Family Day game, he promises a perfect sheet of ice. It won't be easy. The game is two weeks away, and it's a cold, snowy February. Can he and his teammates stick together and do the job, no matter what?